JIM'S DOG MUFFINS

story by
Miriam Cohen

pictures by
Lillian Hoban

A Young Yearling Book

Published by
Dell Publishing
a division of
Bantam Doubleday Dell Publishing Group, Inc.
1540 Broadway
New York, New York 10036

ISBN: 0-440-44224-9

Reprinted by arrangement with William Morrow and Company, Inc.

Printed in the United States of America

May 1986

15   14   13   12   11   10   9   8   7

WES

FOR DR. EDITH WEIGERT—
"NATURE WILL SAY,
'DON'T CRY ANYMORE.' "

"Jim's dog got killed by the garbage truck!
It was all squashed!
Jim's not coming to school today."
Danny was telling everybody about it.

"Did Jim cry?" Paul asked.

"No," Danny said. "But he wouldn't talk to anybody."

Their teacher said, "Jim must be very sad.
If we write a letter to him,
it may help him feel better."

The teacher wrote what they said.

Dear Jim,
We wish Muffins didn't die. She was a nice dog.
Love,
ANNA MARIA
DANNY
SAMMY
SARA
PAUL
LOUIE
MARGARET

After school, the teacher took the letter
to Jim's house.

When Jim came back, he wouldn't talk to anybody.
That morning they gave their whale reports.
Louie said, "Whales will never bite you."

And Paul said that whales can even sing.
But Jim wasn't listening.
He was thinking about Muffins.

The home-making teacher came in with bags of carrots, onions, parsley, and potatoes. "We're going to cook vegetable soup today." She showed them how to cut up everything into small pieces.

Anna Maria said, "Danny is throwing
big pieces in!" Everybody was waiting
for the soup to be cooked, except Jim.
He was looking out the window.

When the soup was ready, they invited
the principal to have lunch with them.
They sat down at the table and the
principal and the teacher started to eat.
"Oh, this is so good!" they said.

But Danny said, "There is something in here!
What is it? Yech! Parsley!"
And he began to take every piece of parsley
out of his soup. By the time he got it all out,
lunch was over.

In the playground, Jim sat on a bench.
Louie and Sammy came over to see him.
"Maybe you'll forget Muffins, Jim?"
Jim shook his head.

Danny put his arm around Jim,
"Don't worry," he said. "I'm never going to die."
Jim didn't say anything.

Anna Maria sat down on
the bench next to Jim.
"It doesn't do any good
to be sad," she said.

Jim yelled, "Shut up! Get away!"
And he pushed Anna Maria off the bench.

Anna Maria started screaming. When the teacher came, she cried, "I was just trying to make him feel better!"

The teacher said,
"Maybe Jim needs time
to feel sad."

Jim stayed by himself. If anybody
came near, he put his hands on his ears.
And Anna Maria told them,
"Don't play with him."

Jim didn't even choose a book
when it was time for the whole
school to stop and read. He just sat.

After school Jim
started home again.

Paul ran after him. "My father
gave me money for two slices
of pizza. Come on, Jim."
"I don't want any," Jim said.

The pizza smell came around the corner.
When they came to the store, Paul stopped.
"Two slices, please," he said.

He gave one to Jim.
Jim just held it.
Then Paul did what they always did.
He pushed a lot of pizza into his mouth.

Jim looked at Paul. He took one bite.
Then he began pushing pizza in.
They began to laugh.
They laughed and laughed.

Jim said, "Remember how I used to give
Muffins the crust?"
Tears came down on his pizza,
but he kept on eating.

"She was the nicest dog,"
Paul said.
"Yes," said Jim.
And they walked home together.